Summer Showdown

OTHER YEARLING BOOKS
YOU WILL ENJOY:

YEARLING BOOKS/YOUNG YEARLINGS/YEARLING CLASSICS are designed especially to entertain and enlighten young people. Patricia Reilly Giff, consultant to this series, received the bachelor's degree from Marymount College. She holds the master's degree in history from St. John's University, and a Professional Diploma in Reading from Hofstra University. She was a teacher and reading consultant for many years, and is the author of numerous books for young readers.

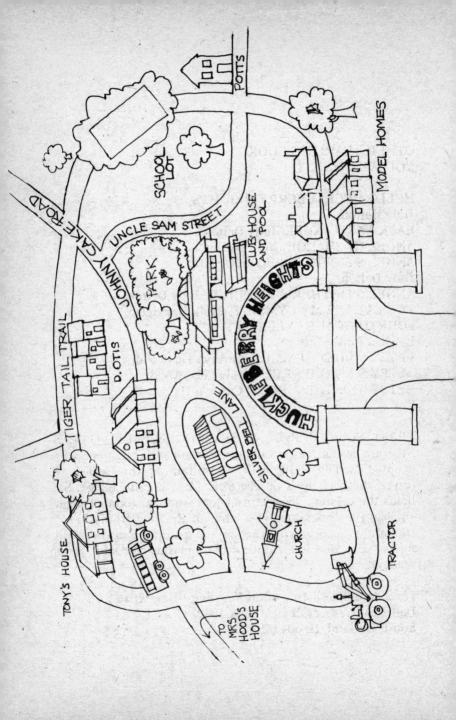

THE CONDO KIDS

Summer
Showdown

Judy Delton

Illustrated by Alan Tiegreen

A YEARLING BOOK

Published by
Dell Publishing
a division of
Bantam Doubleday Dell Publishing Group, Inc.
666 Fifth Avenue
New York, New York 10103

ISBN: 0-440-40307-3

Printed in the United States of America

July 1990

10 9 8 7 6 5 4 3 2
CWO

For Joan Pierce, with whom I share native St. Paulism, Native Catholicism, and native St. Catherinism. We both like to write too.

And with thanks to Lori Mack, editor extraordinaire.

1

"We live in the best place on the whole consonant," said Edgar.

"A consonant is a letter," I said. "Like *c* or *d* or *z*."

Edgar shook his head. "It's a bunch of countries."

Edgar's father is a professor. Their family does funny things with words. Sometimes they rhyme things when they talk.

"A continent is a piece of land," I said. "Like North America."

1

Edgar didn't look convinced.

We were sitting on my front steps. We live in a pink condo in Huckleberry Heights. Our address is number 15 Tiger Tail Trail. The condos look like big houses on the outside, but inside they are separate homes for four families. We are the only ones in our building so far because it's brand-new.

My name is Tony Doyle, and I'm ten. I have a sister, Marcy, who's twelve, and a brother, Gus, who is eight.

Edgar poked at the mud with a stick. "I'm glad school is done," he said. "This summer we'll have lots of fun."

Our front door opened and my mom came out with her toolbox and a pipe and a faucet and a thing that looked like a mailbox.

"It's time we had a suitable mailbox," she said. "You and Edgar can help."

We followed my mom down the muddy lawn. We're getting grass but it isn't in yet.

2

"Screwdriver," said my mom. "Wrench. Washer."

We handed them to her.

After about a half hour she was through, and our mailbox sat on a fancy stand. On top sat a shiny faucet. You could turn it on but no water came out.

"It's subliminal advertising," said my mom, standing back to admire her work.

That's my mom's business, faucets. She owns Trixie's Taps. They make and sell decorator faucets. "Goldtone, silver, porcelain, or pewter?" she says to customers, just like a waitress saying "Coffee, tea, or milk?"

"I'd rather have a big sign in the front yard," she said. "But this will have to do."

Signs were forbidden in Huckleberry Heights. No advertising. For aesthetic reasons.

"No one can complain about this," she went on. "It's really a piece of art."

My mom made sculptures out of her

old faucets. We had them all over the house.

When she went back into the house, Gus and his friend Lenny Fox came out. Lenny had a glass jar with a bee in it, and a dandelion.

"Hey, look! He's trying to marinate the flower!" shouted Edgar.

"Ha," I laughed. "Yeah, he's marinating it and then he's going to put it on the grill. Barbecued dandelion, yum-yum."

"You mean pollinate," said Lenny. He's only eight but he is smart. "Marinate is what you do to steak. You soak it in oil and vinegar and spices."

We all sat around and watched this bee pollinate. Then Marcy and her friend Daisy Otis came out and watched with us. Talk about boring. I was glad school was out, but I wondered what we'd do all summer in Huckleberry Heights. Three months could be one giant yawn.

"Children," called my mother from an upstairs window. "I have something to discuss. We'll have a family meeting in the Oval Room in a half hour."

We froze. I could almost see Gus's hair stand on end. Marcy had a wild look in her eye, and I think the corner of her mouth twitched. My mom's meetings meant some kind of trouble.

Our living room wasn't oval—it was rectangular. But Mom made a big thing of these meetings, and she said if the President could meet in an oval room, so could she.

In a half hour we were all in the living room, including Daisy and Lenny and Edgar, and our sheepdog, Smiley. We dragged kitchen chairs in because my mom likes us in rows. I put the fern stand in front so she would have somewhere to put her notes.

When she came in, she rapped on the fern stand with a little rubber hammer. "Will the meeting please come to order, and may we have the minutes of the last meeting," she said.

Daisy read them. Then Mom said, "I have called you all together today to discuss summer. What to do with it. How to plan it. Where to spend it. And mainly, who might waste it."

We all clapped. Not because we wanted to talk about summer, but because my mom loved applause.

"I will open the meeting to suggestions from the floor."

"I want to play," said Gus.

"The chair does not recognize those who speak without raising their hand," said my mother.

An hour ago I had been worried about a boring summer. Now something even worse was going to happen. My mom was going to plan our summer for us.

Marcy raised her hand and said she had to baby-sit.

Then Edgar raised his hand.

"The chair recognizes Edgar Allan

Potts," said my mother, who reminded me of Judge Wapner.

"My dad says that free time nurtures creativity. He says plans and activities turn children into robots and stifle original thought."

We all clapped loudly.

"Edgar's father is a *professor*!" I said.

"We wouldn't want to stifle creativity," said my mother.

We all clapped again. Lenny whistled through his teeth.

"But on the other hand," she went on, "idle hands are the devil's playhouse."

"Workshop, Mom," corrected Marcy. My mom always got sayings wrong.

"Now that you have spoken," said my mom, "I will tell you my idea. I have a program here from our new clubhouse."

She waved a brochure at us.

"It offers fine classes to keep you busy and improve your minds. Right here in our own backyard. I want to see your talent bloom."

"I hate arts and crafts!" whined Marcy. "I don't want to weave baskets."

"We go to school all year," I said. "We don't want classes in summer."

But my mom hit the fern stand with the hammer. We knew when we were licked.

"Will someone move that we adjourn?" she said.

"Arf arf arf!" barked Smiley.

"I second that motion," said Lenny.

"It has been moved and seconded that we adjourn our meeting," said my mother.

But by that time we were out the door.

"It won't be so bad," said Lenny. "We'll have fun making stuff at the clubhouse."

"Are you going?" shrieked Gus.

"My dad is making me," Lenny answered.

"So is mine," said Edgar. "My mom is teaching one of the classes."

Parents were all alike. My mom just seemed worse because she was so showy.

9

We read the brochure. "Have an enriching Huckleberry summer!" it said. "Come to our new clubhouse and learn."

"I'm taking Create a Play," said Edgar. "My mom is making me. She teaches it."

That sounded like as much fun as anything listed. At least I'd be with Edgar. I hoped his mom wouldn't make us memorize stuff.

Marcy and Daisy were taking Make It with Beads. "Make gifts for your friends. Headbands, watchbands, rings, wastebaskets. Bead your way to a happy Huckleberry summer!"

Gus and Lenny decided to sign up for French lessons.

We decided we'd better play the rest of the weekend. Classes started on Monday. We rode bikes around Tiger Tail Trail and up Johnny Cake Road, where Lenny lives. We rode by the model homes and the clubhouse. We checked out new people who had moved in, to see if there were any new kids, and we played Nuclear Holocaust in one of the sand pits where a foundation was going in. It was a game I had taught them, where you try to find one living thing on the face of the earth. It isn't easy in a sand pit.

And then it was Monday. Poor Edgar. How embarrassing it must be to have your mother teach a class. Especially a class that you are in.

When we got to the clubhouse, we looked around a little. We had watched the thing go up, right from the very first brick they put in.

"Today's the plaster!" Lenny would shout, and we'd go and watch. Then they poured the cement for the swimming pool, all wet and slithery and shiny.

It was hard to believe all that wet stuff could get so hard and we'd be swimming in that pool soon.

Another day we watched them put

tile down around the pool. Over the pool was this big glass dome that let the sun in even when there was snow on the ground. It would be like swimming in Florida instead of Minnesota. In summer it opened up to let the fresh air in.

"Boy, this place is fancy!" said Edgar.

"It's the best clubhouse in St. Paul," said Daisy Otis.

It smelled brand-new. The classes were the first things going on there. It was so big, it felt like we were in church. I felt like whispering.

Gus and Lenny found the French room, and Marcy and Daisy found the bead room, and Edgar and I found Create a Play.

Edgar pretended to be brave. We opened the door to Mrs. Potts's class, and Edgar said, "Let's sit in the front row."

When all the chairs were filled and we settled down, the door opened and the teacher walked in. I couldn't believe my eyes. It wasn't Mrs. Potts who stood in the front of the room smiling. Instead of "poor Edgar" it was "poor me."

The teacher of Create a Play was my very own mother.

"**I** forgot to tell you my mom got sick," said Edgar on the way home.

We were still wearing our gladiator suits and carrying our swords. I was in such a hurry to get out of there, I didn't take my costume off.

"She got so nervous about teaching that she broke out in a rash," Edgar went on, pretending to fence with a little sapling.

"So she's coming tomorrow?" I asked.

Edgar shook his head. "When she

thinks about coming, she starts to itch again. The doctor said she has to cancel."

I felt like itching. I'd have more than a rash if I had to go to school with my mother.

Marcy and Daisy ran to catch up with us. They were wearing beaded headbands.

"Those are cool," said Edgar.

Why wasn't I in a class called Make It with Beads?

"Hey, Tony, your girl friend is in our class," said Daisy.

"You know," said Marcy, rolling her eyes. "Lily Camp."

I tried to act as if I didn't know her.

Lily had been in my room at school. She sat across from me the first day. The second day she'd brought me a notebook with a red heart on it, and the third day she'd kissed me on the playground. I hate her.

"Hey, wait up," called a voice from behind us.

Lily was all out of breath from running after us. After me.

Her curls were bouncing and her cheeks were pink. She *was* cute.

She reached into the pocket in her jeans and fished something out.

"I made this for you, Tony," she said. "It's a genuine beaded ring. It was a lot of work."

She grabbed my hand and jammed it on my finger.

Edgar and the girls were making snickering noises and trying to pretend they weren't laughing.

I wanted to say, Get lost and take your ring with you. But that isn't a nice thing to say to someone who gives you a present.

Lily hung on my arm all the way down Tiger Tail Trail, and I couldn't shake her loose.

"You look so handsome in that suit," she said. I suppose I did. It made me

17

look strong. Girls like strong guys. I flexed my muscles.

When we got to my house, I shook Lily off and dashed inside.

"Why are you teaching that class?" I yelled to my mother. "You have to go to work."

"I took some time off, Tony," she said. "It was an emergency. A person has to take community responsibility. And the rule is to leave your costume in the classroom closet."

Lenny and Gus came in spouting French words.

The next morning I tried to get into the French class, but it was full.

I tried to get into Make It with Beads, and it was full too.

There was a waiting list for every class. Just when I felt doomed, Punkin Head Mahoney (he's in Gus's class) took me aside at the water fountain in the clubhouse.

"Psst," he said. "I hear you've got a

19

problem. You need to get out of Create a Play?"

I nodded.

"I think I can help," he said. "We'll change classes. I'll go to your class, and you can go to mine. We'll switch."

It couldn't be that easy. Punkin Head had a reputation for shrewd dealings.

He leaned against the wall with his chubby arms folded. "You can go to Know Your Garden. I hate dirt and weeds and stuff. I always wanted to be in a play."

I reached my hand out to shake on it, but Punkin Head had two sticky hands from the doughnut he was eating.

"It's a deal!" I said.

The teacher in Know Your Garden didn't take attendance. His name was Mr. Custer. He didn't seem to care that I had switched. Or else he just thought I was Punkin Head. But how could he? Punkin Head was a lot fatter than I am.

My mom was another matter. "Punkin Head wanted to take your class," I said. "And he couldn't get in. It was the least I could do."

"That was very generous," said my mom.

"*Oui, oui,*" said Gus. "That means yes, yes."

"Arf!" barked Smiley. He was wearing a beaded collar with his name on it.

"I can learn all about gardens so I can plant some flowers in ours," I said. Every condo in Huckleberry Heights had a little garden plot for the people who wanted to grow their own vegetables or flowers. The association cut the grass, but the people had to tend their own gardens.

"Some marigolds would be nice," mused our mother. "It would add some color to our yard."

"The teacher said petunias are the best all-around annual for our climate," I said. "They come in pink, to match our house. Marigolds look best in autumn."

My mom looked impressed. "Petunias will be fine," she said.

The next day I came home with a plant book.

Marcy came home with a beaded toaster cover.

And Gus came home with French vowels to learn.

All week after classes Edgar and I and Gus and Lenny and Punkin Head watched the men lay sod. We watched the sewer pipes go in where the new condos were being built. And we climbed on the big yellow tractors that were digging up the street. We called our street Dinosaur Street because there were so many big machines on it.

"They put down asphalt on Silver Bell Lane today!" reported Edgar. "I'll bet Tiger Tail Trail will be next."

Edgar and I ran down to Silver Bell and put our footprints in the soft, hot asphalt in front of the church.

E.A.P. wrote Edgar next to his print. "The name Edgar Allan Potts will live forever in this tar," he said.

I decided to put my handprint in the street. I took a stick and traced around my fingers so it would be clear. Nice and deep. Underneath I wrote *Anthony Doyle put his hand here.*

Edgar and I stood back and looked at it. We felt kind of solemn. Like we should say a prayer or salute or something. Then we went up on the lawn of the churchyard to find out if we could see our prints from far away.

Just when we turned around to look, a big yellow steamroller came down the street and rolled right smack over our prints and squashed them down flat.

"We didn't live forever," said Edgar sadly.

"We didn't even last for five minutes!" I cried.

"They're pouring cement by the fire station next week," said Edgar. "That will be better anyway. It's more permanent."

My mom came home with some packages of petunia seeds on Tuesday. "Make us a garden, Anthony," she said.

"It's too late for seeds," I explained. "The best time to plant seeds is early spring. It's summer now. We have to have plants."

"Why, Anthony, you are a real gardener!" she said.

She was right. I'd learned a lot in my class. I knew about fertilizer and perennials and which plants needed the most sun.

"Did you know that poinsettias are poison?" I said to my mother.

"Why, what a useful thing to know!" she said.

"We are hardly going to eat them," scoffed Marcy. "Big deal."

I ignored Marcy. She had on a new beaded bracelet. Everything in the house was beaded lately. Even the wastebasket.

"And monkshood is poison and can be mistaken for purple delphinium."

"Tsk, tsk, tsk," said my mother. "I hope we don't have that in our garden."

When Mom came home from the grocery store, she had a big flat box of pink petunias. "To match our house," she said.

First I spaded up our garden. The dirt was nice and black. My teacher said the blacker the better. I pulled the little plants apart and put them in the garden, a couple of inches apart.

"They looked better closer together," said Gus.

"You can't crowd roots, Gus. By the end of summer this whole garden will be covered with flowers."

Gus looked doubtful.

"Yuck, I hate dirt," said Daisy, who was watching with Marcy. "It gets under your fingernails and in your pores. It can ruin a manicure."

When I got up to get the hose, I noticed a car in the driveway of the house next door. The condo that was attached to ours. Daisy saw it too.

"Wow!" she said. "That's a fancy car."

It was. It was bright red and had spoked wheels and a low back.

"They must be rich," said Daisy. "My aunt is rich and she drives a car like that."

I turned on the hose, but I couldn't help staring at the condo, and instead of the petunias, I watered Daisy.

28

"Hey, cut it out, Tony Doyle!" she yelled.

"It was a mistake," I said. "I didn't water you on purpose."

Daisy was dripping. Her jeans were soaked and her hair hung like string. I wanted to laugh but I didn't.

She went home to change, and I stored it in my mind as one way to get rid of a girl, like maybe Lily.

I turned the hose off and snuck over to the back door of the condo. I peered in. A lady I couldn't see too well was putting curtains up. As I watched she pulled down a shade and drew the curtains closed, right by my nose. Like she had something to hide. Why wouldn't she want the sunshine to come in her kitchen?

"Mom," I yelled, running in our back door. "We have new neighbors!"

Marcy and Gus came running.

"Have they got kids?" yelled Gus.

"Did you see a baby to sit for?" said Marcy. "Or a cute boy my age?"

"I heard someone bought the place," said my mom.

We all went out in the backyard and watched. But there was nothing to see. It was as quiet as a tomb.

"Maybe I should bake some brownies and take them over," said my mother.

She baked brownies, but we ate them. She went next door, but no one answered the doorbell when she rang.

"They must be there." She frowned. "The car is in the drive."

Gus finished off the last brownie.

"Oh, well," she said. "They may be sleeping. They are all worn out from moving day."

"I didn't see a moving van," said Marcy.

That night I heard noises on the other side of my wall. Pushing and scraping noises. I snuck into Marcy's room and told her.

We both put our ears against the wall

of my bedroom to listen. We couldn't hear much more.

"Hey," said Gus. We jumped a foot.

"If you put a glass against the wall and put your ear on the glass, you can hear," he said.

He ran to the kitchen and got a drinking glass and showed us. Sure enough! We could hear better.

"Let me," whispered Marcy.

"Someone is talking," she said. "It sounds like they said ride the honey. Or maybe, hide the money!"

Marcy looked at me. I looked at Gus. We were all thinking the same thing.

"Thieves!" said Gus.

"Criminals!" said Marcy. "Right next door."

I didn't want to jump to hasty conclusions. All we knew was that they were rich, drove a fancy car, pulled their curtains so no one could see in, didn't answer the door when the bell rang, and

said, "Hide the money," in the middle of the night.

"We can't be sure," I said. "We'll need more evidence."

All night I didn't sleep. I thought I could hear them sawing a hole in my wall and coming through and taking my bank off my desk. I got up and took their advice, I hid my money. I put it on the floor in my closet, underneath my backpack.

In the morning the red car was gone.

After my plant class there was a blue car there.

"Maybe they steal cars," said Gus.

"Anybody can have two cars," I said. But I warned my mom to lock the garage.

"Pooh," said my mother. "There are no burglars in Huckleberry Heights."

I shot a warning glance at Gus. No use worrying my mother until we had real evidence.

After class we rode bikes around,

watching the school go up and sod get laid. I told Lenny and Edgar and Punkin Head about our new neighbors.

They got on their bikes and started toward my house right away.

"Hey, guys! We can't go snooping around in broad daylight," I said.

"Tonight," said Lenny. "We'll meet you at nine."

The guys came early. "I have to be home by dark," said Edgar.

The sun was almost down. It was good enough. My family was watching TV and I snuck out the back door.

Lenny was taking notes. *Blue Honda,* he wrote down. *Brand-new.*

We walked around the house to the windows. The curtains were pulled. We could only see shadows. One window didn't have a curtain, and there was a light on. But it was too high to reach.

"Get a ladder," ordered Punkin Head.

"My mom will hear me if I go in the garage," I said.

We looked around for something to stand on. Edgar found an old box in the yard. He shoved it under the window.

Lenny found a log and put it on top of the box.

"It's still not high enough," I said.

Punkin Head ran home and came back with a step stool from his kitchen. He piled it on top of the log.

"Who is going to climb it?" I asked.

"It's your neighbor," said Edgar.

"You have the longest legs," said Lenny.

"I'll hoist you," said Punkin Head, giving me a shove.

"I don't like this," I said. "I think it's illegal."

"The police will thank us," said Lenny. "It's our civic duty to protect Huckleberry Heights."

By that time the three guys had shoved me up and I was on the top step of the stool.

"I can't see anything," I said. "We need binoculars."

"Take Edgar's glasses," said Lenny.

Lenny passed the glasses up to me. Edgar didn't look happy about letting me use them.

I put the glasses on and looked in the window. Now everything was real blurry. All of a sudden I felt dizzy. I swayed to the side and the stool began to wobble. I grabbed at the window frame but it was too late. Out of nowhere I heard a familiar voice.

"Anthony! Where in the world are you? It's getting dark, get home this minute!"

My mother's words exploded in the quiet summer night air like a bomb.

Crash! The stool and log and box gave way and I hit the ground with a bang. When I opened my eyes, the guys were gone.

I was glad to find that Edgar's glasses weren't broken. They were just bent.

I limped around the corner of the house. When I saw my mom, I quit limping. I could feel a lump on my head get bigger. I combed a lot of my hair over it.

My mom was eager to get back to her TV program. She didn't look at me very closely. I hobbled up the steps to my room and fell onto my bed.

"That's it," I said out loud to myself. "I don't care who lives there. I am going to forget it. Bonnie and Clyde can live there for all I care."

In the morning I took a hot bath to loosen my muscles, and went to plant class.

We looked at plant leaves under a microscope. Then we identified wild-flowers.

"Be careful never to eat the berry of this plant," said Mr. Custer. "It may look like a good berry to eat, but it is deadly."

Nature was tricky. There were lots of poison plants. Even the plant in our living room was poison, my mom's dieffenbachia.

"Hey, you guys, you sure ran off fast last night," I said to Edgar and Lenny and Punkin Head after class.

I handed Edgar his glasses. He put them on, but they were cockeyed. One side was real high and the other was real low.

"Your mom came," said Lenny.

"Fine friends you are," I muttered.

"We knew you were okay," said Edgar.

"I wasn't. Look at this bump on my head."

The guys looked. Punkin Head felt it. "I had a bigger one than that one time," he said.

"We've got to have a stakeout," said Lenny. "I drew up plans on paper."

"No way," I said. "I'm through with snooping."

I ran to catch up with Marcy and Gus. "Look at the wallet I made," said Marcy. "Daisy made a lampshade for her room."

Then I went out and watered the petunias, and I didn't even look at the condo next door.

"You'll never guess what," said my mom when I came in the house. "When our classes are over next week, there is

41

going to be a talent show for all the students. You will get to show off the talent you developed in your class."

"Ha," I said. "Should I walk in there with a petunia? Or a leaf from a poison plant?"

"It can be any talent," said my mother. "You have lots of them."

Great. I couldn't think of one. I was a kid without a talent.

Gus burst in the door and said, "I'm going to say a poem in French in the talent show. Do you want to hear it?"

"No," I said.

"Did you hear about the talent show?" asked Marcy when she and Daisy came home. She didn't even wait for me to answer. "We are going to display all of our beadwork. I'll need that belt back that I made for you. Just for the show."

I should have stayed in my mom's class. At least I could have been in some dumb play and memorized a few lines, and they'd clap and it would be over.

"Come on back to the clubhouse," said Gus after lunch. "The new pool is open."

Everyone wanted to try out the pool. Today was the first day it had water in it.

When we got there, there was a sign on the door saying, OPEN SWIM. When we got our suits on, we read another sign that said READ THESE POOL RULES. We did.

The sun was streaming in the hole in the roof, but it was real cool in the water. Lenny was there treading water. Punkin Head was doing the jellyfish float. Edgar was sitting in a chair where it was dry. "I've got allergies to chlorine," he said. "I break out."

I did the dog paddle from one end of the pool to the other. I was really glad we moved to Huckleberry Heights. There was no pool this fancy by our apartment in St. Paul. Gus was paddling away in the shallow end of the pool. The lifeguard was showing him how to float.

"Look at all the kids coming!" said

43

Lenny, taking his nose plug off. "Everybody in Huckleberry Heights is here today!"

"That's because it's the first day," I said.

I heard a big splash beside me, and Marcy and Daisy came up under my chin. Marcy had this black-and-white-striped suit on that made her look like a Zebra. Daisy had a suit with ruffles all over.

"We signed up for water ballet," said Marcy. "We might be in a talent show twice."

"I am too," called Edgar. "I'm going to play the piano, and be in a play."

Great. Some people had talent coming out of their ears. What would I come up with?

I swam up to Punkin Head and asked him what he was going to do for the talent show.

"I don't know yet," he said.

"I don't either," I said. Punkin Head

wasn't too smart in school but he had some good ideas. He could solve problems.

We floated together on our backs, looking up at the dome. It was real peaceful.

All of a sudden I felt someone grab me from underneath and pull me down. I was choking and spluttering when I came up. When I got the water out of my eyes, whoever had done it was gone.

"It was your girl friend," said Punkin Head with this big smile. "Lily Camp."

I started to feel sorry for myself. I still had a lump on my head. I had no talent. And I let a girl duck me under water. I should take a lesson from Bruiser Brady. He's a guy in Marcy's room who scares everybody in the school. I could see him right now throwing kids' towels in the water. I was just too nice a guy.

We played water tag for a while, and I ducked Lily back. No more Mr. Nice Guy, I told her.

"Why are you so mean to her?" hissed Marcy, swimming up to me.

"She's a pest," I said.

"That's because you're so mean to her," Marcy replied.

"I know how you can get rid of her," said Punkin Head, eating a cupcake in the water. I was sure there was a no-eating-in-the-pool rule.

"You act like you don't like her, that's why she bugs you," he said. "Be nice to her and she'll quit bothering you."

When the gong rang and the lifeguard said, "All out," I thought P.H.'s advice was worth a try.

I walked home with Lily. "What are you going to do for the talent show?" I asked.

"Tap-dance," she said.

That didn't surprise me. Lily looked like a tap dancer. I could just see her curls bouncing and her heels clicking.

"How come you're talking to me?"

she asked suspiciously. "You're up to something."

Maybe Punkin Head's advice was working already. She waved to me and ran on to her own house. No red hearts. No kisses. I was going to go out of my way to be nice to Lily.

Just when I got to my door, the red car drove up. I tried not to pay any attention, but out of the corner of my eye I saw a lady get out. She had long white hair like witches have. I would have bet she had missing teeth in front, but I couldn't see that far.

When I got to bed, I fell asleep right away. Swimming is good exercise. All of a sudden I woke up. My heart was beating fast, and I could hear voices. And they weren't in my house. They were outside my window!

I ran over and looked out. The only light was from the moon. My clock said midnight. Someone was out there. I strained my eyes to see. It looked like

the witch was digging in the yard next door. Was she burying something? Was she digging a hole to bury a body? Or a treasure?

I jumped into my jeans right over my pajamas and snuck downstairs real quietly. I let myself out the back door and walked close to the house so no one could see me. If that witch was out there, I didn't want to be under her spell.

At the corner I turned. And then I bumped into something. Something soft. A body.

All of a sudden there was a bloodcurdling yell, and two strong hands grabbed me around my neck.

"**W**hat are you doing out here?" whispered Lenny's voice in my ear. "Now you ruined the whole thing!"

"I live here. What are *you* guys doing out here in the middle of the night?" I said.

"It's a stakeout," said Punkin Head.

I still couldn't see anyone. But the body I felt was Lenny's. And the scream had been his when I stepped on him. The witch who'd been digging in the yard was gone.

"We almost had the criminals," said Punkin Head. "We were just this far from getting them." He held two fingers up to show an itty-bitty space between.

"Somebody was digging out there," said Lenny.

"Well, we can't see anything now. We'll have to look in the morning," I said. I was feeling damp in this night air. "How did you guys get out of the house at midnight?"

"We snuck out the window," said Punkin Head. "Nobody knows we're gone."

"I'll see you in the morning," I said.

I slept late the next day. When I got up, I stretched and looked out the window. There was no witch out there, but there was a surprise. Where the witch had been digging was a garden! An honest-to-goodness garden with things growing in it. Green things. I couldn't believe my eyes.

When I came down to breakfast, my

mom said, "Our new neighbors have a garden too. They must be hard workers."

I stuffed my toast in my mouth and went to call Lenny.

When he and Punkin Head arrived, we took a look at the garden, and Lenny whistled through his teeth. "So that's all they were doing."

"I say it's pretty strange," I said. "Planting a garden in the middle of the night."

I took a close look at the rows of plants.

"This," I said, "looks like monkshood. Our neighbors are raising poison plants."

The guys looked at me as if they were impressed. "And this," I said, pointing to another row, "is marijuana."

"Wow!" said Punkin Head.

"Are you sure?" said Lenny doubtfully.

"Of course I'm sure!" I said. "I'm the smartest one in my plant class. Marijuana has these feathery leaves. This is no ordinary flower garden. They are

53

going to raise these plants till they are big and then sell them!"

"And what are they going to do with the poison ones?" asked Punkin Head.

"I think we all know what poison is for," I said.

The guys seemed to shudder. I hated to tell them we may have honest-to-goodness murderers on our hands. But I think they read my mind.

When I got to plant class, I got Mr. Custer's big reference book of flora and fauna and looked up marijuana. There it was. The plants next door were a lot smaller and lighter green, but they had the same look that the plants in the picture had.

"Psst!" I said to the guys when they came by after class. I took them into the room to look at the picture.

"It does look the same," admitted Punkin Head.

"Maybe," said Lenny. "But what can we do about it anyway?"

I was surprised at Lenny. He was the one who was so hot to track down criminals. Now we had proof, and he sounded half interested.

"We have to meet and discuss this," said Punkin Head. "We need to talk to Edgar and Gus. No girls."

That afternoon everyone went to the pool except us. Punkin Head rounded up Edgar, and I got Gus and we sat in the backyard by Smiley's doghouse and discussed a plan.

Lenny had a notebook. He wrote *Plan* on the first page. "Let's all take a turn saying what we think we should do about this emergency," said Lenny.

No one said anything. We just sat and stared at the marijuana plant leaves blowing in the breeze. And the poison plants sprouting new buds. It was a warm day. A good day for plants to grow.

"Well?" said Lenny. "Who wants to go first? Punkin Head, you start."

"I think we should pull the plants up in the middle of the night when no one can see us," he said.

Lenny wrote that down under number one.

I shook my head. "We can't go on their property and pull up their garden," I said. "That's—vandalism."

"Edgar?" said Lenny. "What do you think?"

"I think we should send a note of warning to them," he said. "One that says, 'We are on to you. Stop or we will report you to the FBI.' Something like that."

Lenny wrote that down under number two. It didn't seem as bad as vandalism.

"Gus?" said Lenny. "It's your turn."

"I think we should tell mom," he said.

"No way," said Punkin Head. "What do grown-ups know about stuff like this? They always make a mess of important things."

Lenny didn't even think it was worth writing down.

It was my turn. "I say we should call the Huckleberry Heights security officers," I said. "Or the police."

I realized when I said it that it sounded like a desperate measure.

"This is our emergency," said Punkin Head. "I don't think we should share it with them. We want to solve it ourselves, and maybe we'll get a medal or something."

While we sat there thinking, the witch came out of the door. She was carrying a box of something heavy. She put it into the trunk of the red car.

"Don't let her see us!" said Punkin Head.

We all scrunched down behind Smiley's doghouse.

As we watched, a man came out. He had a beard. He was carrying two suitcases. They looked heavy.

"I read where some guys snuggle drugs in their beards," said Edgar.

"You mean smuggle," said Gus. "Smuggle drugs."

"He's got drugs in his beard!" said Punkin Head. "I know it!"

We listened. The witch was saying something to the beard. Something about bread.

"Bread is money, in criminal talk," said Lenny.

"There's money in the suitcases!" shrieked Punkin Head.

"I think we need help," I said. "I think it's time to call in the police. These people might be leaving town."

I knew what I had to do. There was no time to waste.

"You keep them in the driveway," I said. "I'm going in to call the police."

"How can we keep them?" asked Punkin Head, jumping up and down. "How can we keep them from leaving?"

"A good detective doesn't ask how— you just do it," I said, disgusted with the way these babies acted in a crisis.

Gus and Edgar stayed by the dog-house to distract the criminals. Punkin Head and Lenny snuck around the house on their stomachs and let the air out of the back tires on the red car. I had to admit, this was teamwork at its best. I had underestimated these guys. Some emergency gland must have switched on in all of us.

I dialed 911 on the kitchen phone.

"Send the police to number sixteen Tiger Tail Trail just as fast as you can. This is an emergency." I hung up and raced outside. The red car was still there.

Lenny and Punkin Head were back behind the doghouse.

"Well done," I said to them. "That took courage. I'll bet you get a medal or something."

"Are the police coming?" said Edgar nervously.

I nodded. "All we have to do now is wait."

The beard had discovered the flat tires.

"He's going to get us," whined Punkin Head. "He's going to poison us or something."

"He doesn't know we did it," I said.

While the beard jacked up the car, the witch took the hose and watered the marijuana and the poison plants. I couldn't believe it! In broad daylight. Like it was a perfectly normal thing to do, watering drug plants.

"Where are the police?" sobbed Punkin Head.

It did seem like ages.

Then just when the beard had got the tires filled with air, and the witch was neatly winding up the hose and putting it on the hose rack, who comes along through our yard trailing her beach bag, but Lily.

"Oh, no," I groaned. "Why now?"

I tried to duck down, but it was too late. She had seen us.

But Lily didn't stop in our yard. She

just waved and ran on. She ran right in front of us, through our backyard and into the yard next door. Number 16 Tiger Tail Trail, the enemy camp.

While we watched she yelled, "Hi, Aunt Jennie!" and threw herself right into the arms of the drug-dealing witch.

Lenny was banging his head on the doghouse in despair. What was this? Was Lily a friend of the criminal's? Worse yet, a relative?

"Maybe she's buying drugs from those guys," said Gus.

"She might just call her 'aunt,' like they do in the mob. One big family," said Edgar.

I just sat there in shock. To think that my girl friend was a member of a drug-smuggling group.

We watched the witch hug Lily. Then she showed her the garden.

"We were going out to get some bread and things," said the witch called Jennie. "But our tires were flat. Two of them, isn't that funny? Why don't you come in and have some lunch with us?"

And then Lily headed for the house. The house with the shades.

But first she caught sight of us all hanging over the doghouse, staring.

"Hey, Aunt Jennie, come and meet my friends!" Lily yelled. "Tony, did you know your new neighbors are my aunt and uncle? I'll be spending a lot of time around your house now," she said to me, batting her eyelashes.

And all of a sudden the witch and beard were standing on our sidewalk, shaking our hands and patting us on the back, saying any friend of Lily's was a friend of theirs, blah, blah, blah.

Then my mother comes out of the

house with an apple pie and gives it to them.

"I never heard of baking an apple pie for somebody before they go to jail," whispered Punkin Head.

The witch's blond hair didn't look as witchy up close. It was long and straight, but Jennie looked more like a hippie than a spook.

And the beard kept rubbing his chin, and no white powder fell out.

Now Mr. and Mrs. Otis were coming up the hill to meet Lily's relatives. Pretty soon we'd be having a block party!

Just when everyone was real chummy and huggy and telling stories about Huckleberry Heights, and Marcy was bringing out some lawn chairs from the garage, we heard the long, low whine of sirens.

I tried to ignore them and hoped it was just a tornado warning. In this hot weather we could have a tornado if that cold Canadian air sent a jet stream down this way.

But it wasn't a tornado. It was the police I'd called. The sirens got louder and louder and the Otises and my mom raised their voices to be heard over them.

"I hope there isn't a fire somewhere," yelled Daisy's mother.

The noise of the siren was earsplitting now. I saw not one, not two, not three, but four squad cars coming down Tiger Tail Trail. Behind them were a lot of other cars that had nothing better to do than follow the police.

Then when the police stopped in front of the house and got out, a fire engine came around the corner with hook and ladder and even a spotted fire dog in the front seat.

"Where's the fire?" shouted Marcy.

A crowd gathered in our yard, and from up and down the block people came running to see what all the excitement was about.

"I didn't know there were this many people in Huckleberry Heights," said Gus.

Lenny and Edgar looked white. They looked as if they were thinking about escaping if they got a chance. But I gave them a warning look and held on to Punkin Head's sleeve. I wasn't in this alone.

"You're the dummy who called the police," said Gus.

The police were pushing their way through the crowd now.

"Stand back! Stand back! Police business!" they were saying over and over.

The firemen were dragging this giant hose through the side yard, and across the neighbor's marijuana plants.

"My garden!" Lily's aunt was saying.

A hush came over the crowd. And then my mother said, "Are you looking for someone?" to the police.

"We had a call," said a policeman. "That there was an emergency at this address."

The crowd murmured and looked around for the emergency. We looked around too. I could see the police were disappointed. When they are called out on an emergency, they like to find one. I decided there was nothing sadder than firemen and a fire dog and a fire truck, all at the ready, and not a fire in sight for miles.

The policeman got a notebook out of his pocket.

"Is this number sixteen Tiger Tail Trail?" he demanded, flipping the pages.

"That's our address," said Lily's aunt. "And we would like to report some strange occurrences—someone let the air out of our tires, right here in the drive-way." She pointed. "And after dark we have been having the feeling we're being watched. Like someone is trying to see in our windows."

The man with the beard agreed with her.

Edgar was turning red.

Wait a minute, I thought. She has it turned around! What is a criminal doing pointing the finger at the good guys?

"Did you call 911?" the policeman asked Jennie.

"No," she said. "I wouldn't call 911 unless the problem was a real emergency."

"Well, someone did," the policeman said.

Suddenly, Gus blurted out, "They are growing marijuana and poison plants in their backyard!"

"And they have money in those suitcases in the red car!" shouted Punkin Head.

"We called 911," I said.

"*You* did," said Lenny. "We wanted to solve it ourselves."

I'll bet there were a million people there, staring at us. All of a sudden a ripple of laughter went through the crowd. It was getting worse and worse.

Take us away, lock us up, give us one hundred lashes, but don't laugh at us!

The policeman was not laughing. The one who'd been doing the talking looked as if he was about to start lecturing.

"Do you know how much tax money it costs to get all this equipment out here, young man?" he said.

"My name is Tony," I said.

Edgar, my friend, stepped forward and put his arm around me. "We were trying to make the world a better place," he said. "I don't think you should laugh at someone who reports a crime."

"Yeah," said Lenny with new courage. "If you do, no one will report crime anymore. And then where would we be?"

"But my aunt and uncle aren't criminals!" shouted Lily.

"Ho!" I said. "Then why are they growing marijuana in their yard?"

"Those are dicentra," said the man. "Commonly known as bleeding hearts."

I couldn't believe my ears. Mr. Custer had a lot of explaining to do.

"If they are just flowers, then why were you sneaking around planting them at midnight?" I asked.

"We always plant by the light of the moon," said Jennie. "Farmers always get better crops when they plant by the light of the moon."

Mr. Custer never told us that, either.

The policeman threw his arms up in the air.

"Then no one has a complaint?" he asked. "This whole thing is a false alarm?"

"Of course it is a false alarm," said my mother. "It was a child's innocent mistake. Let's just go inside and have a cup of coffee and some fresh apple pie and forget the whole thing."

The crowd started drifting off, looking disappointed. We had let them down. There was not even any smoke. The Otises and the new neighbors and the

73

police and firemen went in our kitchen to eat pie, and fill out what the policeman called "routine papers."

No one paid any attention to us.

"My aunt and uncle are not criminals, Tony Doyle," said Lily.

"Well, they look like criminals," muttered Punkin Head.

I thought of one thing good that came of this. Lily wouldn't want me for a boyfriend anymore. No more red hearts and kisses. It was a hard way to get rid of a pest, but it worked.

Edgar and Lenny and Punkin Head started home. Gus went in the house to get some pie. I sat down on the back step and thought about what had gone wrong.

"It *was* kind of a brave thing to do," said Lily.

"I thought you went home."

She moved closer to me on the step.

"I forgive you," she said. "I guess Bud and Jennie do some funny things. Can we still be friends?"

Oh, no. Now there was nothing good that had come from the emergency. I still had a pesky girl friend. And there was a talent show coming up in a few weeks, and I hadn't a single idea in my head of something I could do.

The only thing I'd been good at so far was getting in a lot of trouble.

7

Pretty soon the classes were over, and I hoped my mom wouldn't look for something else for us to do for the summer. Marcy kept beading and Gus kept talking French and I took care of our garden. I even planted some lettuce and we ate it for supper.

The rest of the time we swam at the new pool. The lifeguard gave lessons, and I went from the beginning class to the medium class to the advanced class real fast. I can say, without bragging,

that I was the best swimmer in Huckleberry Heights.

"I could save you if you were drown-
ing," I told Edgar.

"Could you save me, Tony?" said Lily,
sitting down next to me on the edge of
the pool.

I'd never save you, I wanted to say.
You could sink to the very bottom and
I'd swim the other way. But instead I
said, "I s'pose."

Lily came over to see her aunt and
uncle a lot. On the way she'd stop at
our back door and yell my name so
the whole neighborhood could hear.

One morning she brought me a bou-
quet of bleeding hearts from her aunt's
garden. I was embarrassed enough for
having thought they were marijuana;
she didn't have to rub it in.

"Here's some drugs for you, Tony!"
she said, and laughed.

Her aunt's garden was taller and
healthier than mine was—there must

have been something to that planting-by-the-light-of-the-moon business.

Marcy's water show was coming up, and I still hadn't found something to do in the talent show.

"Be a clown," said Marcy. "You could wear a suit and get up there and tell jokes."

"I'm not funny," I said.

"How about juggling," said Daisy. "My cousin could keep four plates up in the air at once. It was hard on her fingernails, though. She kept cracking them."

"The plates?" said Gus.

"Her fingernails, silly," said Daisy. "Well, the plates too. She went through a lot of them before she learned."

"I don't want to juggle," I said.

"You could tap-dance with me," said Lily. "We could be Fred Astaire and Ginger Rogers."

That didn't even deserve a reply.

"Why don't you take piano lessons

real fast," said Edgar. "Then you'd have a talent at last."

"It's too late," I muttered. "The show is next week."

Gus practiced his French poem every day around the house. And Marcy and Daisy practiced for the water show every day from one to three.

"You girls are going to grow scales," said my mom.

The water show was to raise money for the library. My mom bought lots and lots of tickets. Everyone in Huckleberry Heights was going. "We'll sit in the front row," she said.

"Wait till you see the lights," said Marcy. "It starts out perfectly dark, and then colored spotlights shine on the water when we come in."

"Beautiful," said my mom. "We'll be so proud of you."

"I can't wait," said Gus.

I could wait. My sister was a show-off. My mom spent every night sewing

these sequins on one of Marcy's swim-
suits. They had to wear a different suit
for each number.

When the day of the show came,
Marcy and Daisy came running home
from the dress rehearsal crying.

"You'll never guess what," moaned
Marcy. "Tonight is our show and one of
our best swimmers has the measles. Ms.
Swit may have to cancel!"

"After all that practice!" said my
mom. "That would be terrible. Did the
teacher try to find someone else?"

"Everyone who can swim is in it,"
wailed Daisy. "It's too late for anyone
to learn the strokes anyway."

"What does one person matter?" I
said.

"For your information, Tony Doyle, a
water show is precision work. You can't
have a water star without one of the
points. And there would be a big empty
spot in the Niagara Falls number."

They acted like this was really some

big deal. So what, the world could live without a waterfall. Or a star. Daisy's mom came over, and they all looked like they'd cry.

"All those tickets," said my mother. "All that money for the library will have to be returned."

"We have to do something," said Mrs. Otis.

They got on the phone and called every girl in Marcy's class. All of Huckleberry Heights was in a frenzy.

"If I could swim, I'd do it myself," said my aunt Fluffy, who was at our house now too.

"Who do we know who's a good swimmer?" said Daisy.

All of a sudden I could feel them staring at me.

"Ho-ho-ho no," I said. "Don't look at me!"

I backed out of the room, but I wasn't fast enough.

The girls grabbed me. I struggled and

fought, and Marcy yelled, "Mom, make Tony do it! Make him take the part!"

"This is an emergency, Anthony," my mom said.

Emergency was a word I was hearing too often lately. It never meant anything good.

"Come on Tony, pleeeeease!" begged Marcy. She and Daisy were actually down on their knees begging. It was disgraceful.

"I think you should help your sister out," said my mother. "As well as do a great service for your community."

"You'll be a hero!" said Edgar. When did he get here? Was the whole world here to force me into this?

"I can't learn those routines," I said.

"Why not?" said Lenny, who had come to go to the water show with Gus. "You're the best swimmer in Huckleberry Heights."

I had to agree. If anyone could do it, it was me.

My mom called the teacher to tell her the good news.

Marcy and Daisy told me the strokes.

"All you have to do is float with your feet pointed in the middle of this star," said Daisy. "Then we revolve round and round. It's simple."

"And then we tread water in this circle," said Marcy. "Jump up, and dive in. The main thing is that we have to do it all together."

When we got there, Ms. Swit, the teacher, hugged me. "Bless you, Tony," she said. "You have saved our water ballet."

Ballet? This was a *ballet*?

She handed me a pair of red, white, and blue swim trunks. You wouldn't believe it! They had sequins sewn onto them!

"It's a patriotic number," said Ms. Swit. "And you change into these yellow ones for the next piece," she said.

I put the suit on in a closet next to

the girls' dressing rooms. It sparkled all over the place. I looked out, and there in the front row of chairs were my mom and Gus and Edgar and Lenny and Lily and Punkin Head. And a lot of other kids in my room at school. How could I face them in a swimsuit that sparkled?

The rest of the swimmers started to arrive. When they were all there, I noticed something. Something awful. *They were all girls*.

"I'm the only boy?" I shrieked to Marcy.

Marcy and Daisy pretended this was not important. But all the girls in their red, white, and blue suits were snickering and pointing at me.

"Hi, Twinkle Toes," said a girl in my class.

"I am not going to be the only boy in this show!" I yelled.

Ms. Swit gave me a look that said, Save us, Tony. Don't let us down.

Then she started lining us up to go

on, and whispered in my ear, "Just follow the others, Tony, and you'll do fine."

And the next thing I knew, we were lined up along the edge of the pool with our arms around one another's waists, kicking our legs to music that came pouring out of a loudspeaker.

The crowd burst into applause. I didn't know if it was because we were good, or because I looked like a fool.

"Together now!" whispered Ms. Swit. She smiled at me. "The main thing is timing!"

"One two three, one two three!" she called.

There must have been twenty girls in line with me, all in suits with sequins on them, sparkling away, and I was sparkling too.

Then Ms. Swit snapped her fingers, and the first girl in line dropped sideways into the water. The next one followed, and I did the same thing when it

was my turn. We just peeled off that pool like a row of dominoes.

When we hit the water, Ms. Swit called, "Form a star!"

I pointed my toes in the middle of the circle like Marcy said. Then we treaded water, jumped, and dived in a circle.

The colored lights danced on the water, and as we popped up it shone on each of our heads. No one could miss me. I was under a pink spotlight.

"Beautiful!" called Ms. Swit.

She snapped her fingers, and we climbed out of the pool and took a bow and then ran to change for the next act.

"Roller skates?" I shrieked. The girls were all fastening roller skates to their bare feet. Then they went into their dressing room and put on yellow suits.

I put mine on in the closet.

Ms. Swit passed out keys on yellow ribbons to hang around our necks.

"The skates are just to make the entrance," said Daisy. "We take them off before we dive in the water."

Someone started singing, "I've got a brand-new pair of roller skates."

The next thing I knew, we were sailing toward the pool, on wheels. At the edge everyone whipped off the skates in a hurry and dived into the pool.

Everyone, that is, but me. My skate strap caught on a wheel and wouldn't budge. All of a sudden I was in the pool too. Wearing roller skates.

I don't know if you ever tried to swim with roller skates on, but it isn't easy. While the girls swam in formation, I sank. At first my partner lagged behind waiting for me, then she went on on her own. I felt like a treasure chest at the bottom of the sea.

All of a sudden the colored spotlights went off and the bright white pool lights came on. Ms. Swit, instead of snapping her fingers, blew the whistle she had around her neck, and a lifeguard came dashing out of the wings and jumped in to rescue me.

Me, the best swimmer in Huckleberry Heights, had to be fished out of the pool by a lifeguard in the middle of the water ballet while I was wearing trunks with sequins on them. I'd never live this this down.

I wondered if I should pretend to have fainted. I pictured myself hanging limp over the lifeguard's shoulder. Being laid on a towel by the pool with the spotlight on me, while the lifeguard breathed into my mouth as if I were the plastic doll they practiced on. It would be quiet as they watched for some sign of life. Then when I moved my eyelids and took a deep breath, cheers would break out from the throng. They would be so grateful to see me alive, especially my mother (she'd have tears in her eyes), that they would forget how funny I was. Forget to laugh at the boy in sparkly trunks with roller skates on in a swimming pool. Instead, I would be a survivor.

But while I planned this the lifeguard picked me up and put me on his shoulder, and I slid right over him and down his back and into the water again. Those sequins were slippery. It was getting to be a clown act as I got fished out for the second time. The crowd was laughing so hard that I might as well have been wearing a red nose and floppy shoes.

This time the lifeguard made sure he set me down on the floor by the pool. I forgot I still had the skates on, and I lost my balance and went weaving around in circles, trying to stand up.

It was too late to pretend I had fainted.

The girls were out of the water now, and all lined up beside me. The crowd was on its feet whistling and cheering. I wondered if Ms. Swit was going to make us do the roller-skate act again, but it looked like the water ballet

was over. We bowed and left the pool, and Marcy ran up behind me and said, "You were supposed to take the skates off before you jumped in the water, you know."

"I know," I shouted at her. "They got caught."

"Tony, dear!" said Ms. Swit. "You not only saved the show, you made the show! It was wonderful! You are a talented comedian!"

"I wasn't trying to be funny," I said, but Ms. Swit laughed even harder at that.

The lifeguard grabbed me and put me back on his shoulder, and we dashed out for another bow because all the people were shouting, "We want Tony! We want Tony!"

After that, people started to leave, and I was glad to get those yellow trunks off and get into my jeans.

"Ms. Swit says I'm talented," I told my mom on the way home.

"Of course you are, Anthony!" said my mother.

"She thinks I'm funny," I added.

"You are," said Lenny. "Didn't you see everyone howling at you? You should be a stand-up comic."

"The main thing is," said my mother, "you helped the community out in a pinch, and the show brought in a lot of money for the library."

I didn't particularly feel good about being laughed at, but at least I was glad I had some talent. I could swim, and I could be funny. That was better than tap-dancing. It didn't solve my problem of what to do in the talent show, but it made me feel better.

My bed looked tempting to me, even though it was early. Swimming and being funny really tires a person out. I fell asleep and didn't wake up till the sun came in my window and I heard pounding outside.

I looked out, and there was Lily's old aunt pounding away at some sticks in her marijuana garden. Bleeding heart garden, I mean.

After breakfast I went out, and Lily and Gus and Lenny were all helping her make a scarecrow.

"The birds are eating my berries," she said.

The scarecrow looked like a monster. It would scare anyone away. There were some boards nailed together for arms and legs and a body, and it wore Gus's old straw hat and a long plaid shirt that must have been Jennie's or Bud's. Lenny had brought a mop to put on the head for hair.

"My aunt is very creative," said Lily.

"I think she's kind of weird," I whispered back.

"Ho," said Lily. "Just look at the T-shirt she made for me, then." Lily threw out her chest so I could see the

97

big green letters that said LILY across the shirt.

"Did she sew the shirt?" asked Lenny.

"No, silly, she just paints them. Some have pictures and some have names."

That gave me an idea. I walked up to Jennie.

"Is it hard to paint on a shirt?" I asked.

"No," said Jennie. "It's a lot of fun. If you want to come over this afternoon, I'll show you how I do it."

"Can I come?" said Gus.

"Sure," said Jennie. "All of you can come."

By the time we were ready to go, Marcy and Daisy found out about it and wanted to come too.

"I'm going to get Edgar and Punkin Head," said Gus.

The guys didn't lose any time when they heard we were going to get inside the mystery house.

When we got there, Jennie had her

hair tied back with a scarf. She looked kind of cute, a little bit like Lily. Nothing in the house seemed spooky. The shades were up now, and except for a lot of plants around in pots, and some great big paintings of things I couldn't identify, the house looked a lot like ours.

"My uncle Bud did those abstract paintings," said Lily.

"Can't he make things look real?" asked Punkin Head.

"He can, but he doesn't want to," replied Lily.

"I'll bet," muttered Gus. "I'll bet he does those circles and squares because he can't draw dogs or cows or stuff."

"We'll go downstairs to my workroom," said Jennie.

We followed her. She showed us all these T-shirts that were really neat. Some had HOT STUFF painted on them.

And some had flowers and frogs and sayings.

She showed us great big tubes of these juicy, squishy paints, really bright and shiny. It made you want to put your hands right in them and smear them around, they were so slippery and slidy. But Jennie said we had to use a brush.

"I'll show you how it works," she said. "And then you can try it."

She mixed the shiny paints on a big plate. Gobs of them. Round and round till she got a pretty pink color. Then she showed us how she made the brush marks that looked like a pink rose.

"It takes a while to dry, but then you can wash the shirts over and over and the acrylic paint stays on," she said.

She let us practice on pieces of paper. "When you get a real good picture, you

can put it on a T-shirt to wear," she said.

Marcy and Daisy were really excited. They decided to make shirts alike. They painted ballet shoes in the middle and then their names under them.

Lily made one for her mother that had a heart on it and said MOM. Thank goodness she didn't put *my* name on it.

Lenny painted a race car, and Edgar made something that rhymed and Gus painted a picture of Smiley. The only way you knew it was Smiley was that it said his name under it.

I didn't paint on mine at all. What I wanted to do was a secret. I didn't want Marcy or Gus to see it. Or Lily or Edgar or Lenny or Punkin Head.

I went up to Jennie. "Do you suppose," I said, "I could take my shirt and a little paint home with me?"

"Of course," said Jennie.

"I watched you and I know how to do

it," I said. "But I want mine to be a surprise."

I folded my T-shirt and put a little bit of paint in a pill bottle that Jennie gave me.

"Tell us!" demanded Marcy. "Tell us what you are going to paint on yours!"

"It's not fair," said Gus. "You saw ours!"

"You'll see," I said. "You'll see when I'm finished."

I couldn't wait to get home. I had things to buy. Painting to do. And it was all going to be my great big giant secret.

9

When I got home, I went right to my room and shut my door tight. I got out an old paintbrush and my ruler, and I measured the letters I wanted to put on the T-shirt. I was real careful to get them straight and tall, and I wrote what I wanted to say in pencil first. Then I painted it blue.

When I finished, I let it dry, and then I turned the shirt over and wrote two long words on the back. I painted them on in red.

"What are you doing in there?" yelled Gus.

"Stay out!" I said. My mom didn't let us have locks on our doors because once when Gus was little, he locked himself in his room and the fireman had to come and climb up a ladder to get him out.

I hung the shirt in the very back of my closet and cleaned up the paints. Then I shook my bank till all the money came out, and took my birthday money out of my underwear drawer and my allowance out of my desk.

There was a new mall called Yankee Doodle Mall going up right outside Huckleberry Heights. So far there were only a couple of stores open. What I needed I could get at the store that was open, so I got my bike out of the garage and yelled to Marcy.

"I'll be right back! I'm going to the mall."

I rode off before Gus could yell, "I want to come too."

I found just what I needed when I got there. Some plain white T-shirts and some paints just like Jennie's in lots of bright colors. I got a new brush, and I got the shirts in Large.

When I got home I snuck in the house through the garage with my big package. Marcy was starting supper, and Gus was giving Smiley a bath.

I went to my room and measured and drew and painted. My arm got stiff after a while, and I had to take a break, (While I relaxed I put a glass up to the wall and put my ear on it. Just checking.) The next day I painted some more. The guys kept coming to the door and Lily called me on the phone, but I had a job to do. When I had finished, I could take up my social life again.

The talent show was getting closer. Everybody was practicing for it. Lily wore her tap shoes all the time and even practiced on our sidewalk. Marcy had lots of beaded things to show.

"I'll bet you could sell those at the show," said Aunt Fluffy one afternoon. "I know I'd buy that beaded cosmetic bag."

Aunt Fluffy and my mom were in charge of setting up tables at the talent show and making sure the piano stool was at the piano. That kind of thing.

Edgar's dad was in charge of refreshments afterward, and Lenny's mother was taking care of the lights.

"I told my mom to keep the spotlight right on me the whole time," said Lenny.

"Have you decided what you are going to do for the talent show?" asked my mom the day before the show. I imagine she was nervous, but she didn't want to pressure me.

"Yes," I said. "You'll see when we get there."

Marcy looked nervous too. "Maybe we should see it first," she said. "You could bomb, you know."

"I won't," I said.

I wandered over to Edgar's house. He was pounding away at the piano like a madman. I had to put my hands over my ears.

"It's Chopin," he said. "It has to be loud."

Edgar's mother was making strawberry jam in the kitchen.

"My mom is going to take her reserves to the talent show," said Edgar.

"You mean preserves," I said. "I didn't know grown-ups could be in the talent show."

"No one said they couldn't," said Edgar.

It's good my mom and Aunt Fluffy didn't know that. My mom would surely have had all her faucets on display. She might have even given a talk about them. It was a close call.

When it was time to leave for the show, I got my things together in a big bag. Gus kept saying his French poem over and over. Marcy was carrying all her beaded stuff in a ballet bag.

Lily was the first one onstage. She really looked cute tapping away in her little ruffly dress. I clapped and clapped. Then right at the end when she was doing this fancy step, she tripped and fell. I clapped even louder. I knew what it felt like to make a fool of yourself.

"Yea, Lily!" I said, and whistled between my teeth.

"Why, just look at that," I heard my mom say to Aunt Fluffy. "Mrs. Potts has her strawberry preserves set up for sale! If I'd known that, I could have brought my faucets."

"Tony, why didn't you tell us that grown-ups could be in the talent show?" asked Aunt Fluffy.

"I didn't know," I said truthfully. I really didn't know. Until this morning.

Gus forgot three lines of his French

poem, but no one knew the difference because they couldn't understand French.

Marcy's beaded things went like hotcakes. So did Daisy's. Now every house in Huckleberry Heights would be beaded, not just ours.

And then it was my turn. No one knew what my talent was. I was the only surprise. I got onstage and the spotlight was on me. I opened my bag and arranged the T-shirts on the table. Then I held one of them up for the people to see. Each letter on the front and the back of the shirt was painted a different color. The shirt really was an eye-catcher.

"Our new neighbor, Jennie, taught me how to do this," I said. Then I told about how you have to practice on paper, and measure and let the paint dry and everything. There were lots of questions.

Everyone wanted to know where to get the acrylic paint that was just made

for T-shirts. I told them. When I was through, everyone clapped and yelled and came dashing up, and in five minutes every single T-shirt I painted was gone. I got back all the money I spent, and lots more. I wished I'd made a million more shirts.

"Where did you ever get this idea?" asked Aunt Fluffy.

"Anthony, you have all kinds of talents," said my mom proudly.

She was wearing one of my T-shirts. So were Aunt Fluffy and Lily and Bud and Jennie and Marcy and Daisy. The large size hung down pretty far on Gus and Lenny, but they looked cool anyway.

"I don't have one for myself," I said.

It was true. I was the only one of my friends and family who was not wearing a shirt that said THE CONDO KIDS on the front of it and HUCKLEBERRY HEIGHTS on the back. Under the HUCKLEBERRY HEIGHTS there was a bunch of huckleberries. I found a picture of them in the plant book I'd used in my class. I found out they really had grown in Huckleberry Heights before all the houses went up.

"Are you sure this isn't marijuana, Tony?" said the policeman who'd talked to us at our house that day I dialed 911. He pointed to the berries on his shirt. It turned out he lived in Huckleberry Heights himself. His kids went to my school.

Everyone laughed. I didn't mind. Being funny is one of my talents.

After all the talent was over, we ate the snacks Mr. Potts had fixed.

"I didn't know you were such a businessman," Punkin Head said to me while we were eating. "You could make a million dollars in the T-shirt business."

"I don't want to go into business," I said. "I'll just make some more for the kids in Huckleberry Heights."

"My mom and dad want one," said Lily.

"So do mine," said Lenny.

"What a creative mind you have, Anthony," said my mom in the car on the way home. "You see what a good thing those summer classes were—all of you developed your talents."

I wanted to tell her I didn't learn how to paint T-shirts in my plant class. And Gus was no big expert on French. But I didn't. It's important to let parents think they know more than we do.

When we got home, my mom stretched out on the couch. Marcy was beading some new bags. Gus threw a ball for Smiley to catch.

"You know, Tony," said my aunt Fluffy, looking at her new T-shirt in the mirror. "You should really sign the T-shirts, like artists do."

"*Oui, oui,*" said Gus.

My mom yawned. "I'm so glad we

moved to Huckleberry Heights," she said. "We really found our shelf."

"Niche, Mom," said Marcy. "We found our niche."

"Yes, we did," she replied.

CELEBRATING

YEARLING
25 YEARS

Yearling Books
celebrates its
25 years—
and salutes
Reading Is
Fundamental®
on its 25th
anniversary.